NORTH AMERICA

ANNETTE
WHIPPLE

Rourke
Educational Media

Before & After Reading Activities

Before Reading:

Building Academic Vocabulary and Background Knowledge

Before reading a book, it is important to tap into what your child or students already know about the topic. This will help them develop their vocabulary, increase their reading comprehension, and make connections across the curriculum.

1. *Look at the cover of the book. What will this book be about?*
2. *What do you already know about the topic?*
3. *Let's study the Table of Contents. What will you learn about in the book's chapters?*
4. *What would you like to learn about this topic? Do you think you might learn about it from this book? Why or why not?*
5. *Use a reading journal to write about your knowledge of this topic. Record what you already know about the topic and what you hope to learn about the topic.*
6. *Read the book.*
7. *In your reading journal, record what you learned about the topic and your response to the book.*
8. *After reading the book complete the activities below.*

Content Area Vocabulary
Read the list. What do these words mean?

canals
colonies
descendants
indigenous
industry
lichen
plantations
temperate
textiles
tourism

After Reading:

Comprehension and Extension Activity

After reading the book, work on the following questions with your child or students in order to check their level of reading comprehension and content mastery.
1. What are some examples of the variety of life in North America? (Summarize)
2. Why are cloud forests important? (Infer)
3. Why did European countries build colonies in North America? (Asking Questions)
4. How does the tundra compare to where you live? (Text to Self Connection)
5. How does the Panama Canal help you and your family? (Synthesize/Evaluate)

Extension Activity
Compare a population map and a physical map of North America. What countries are the most populated? Compare the size of the countries to the number of people who live there. Where do the fewest people live? Where do the most people live? If possible, use Google Earth to explore North America's geography and special features.

TABLE OF CONTENTS

Countries in North America:

- Antigua and Barbuda
- Bahamas
- Barbados
- Belize
- Canada
- Costa Rica
- Cuba
- Dominica
- Dominican Republic

- El Salvador
- Grenada
- Guatemala
- Haiti
- Honduras
- Jamaica
- Mexico
- Nicaragua
- Panama

- Saint Kitts and Nevis
- Saint Lucia
- Saint Vincent and the Grenadines
- Trinidad and Tobago
- United States of America (U.S.A. or U.S.)

WELCOME TO NORTH AMERICA

North America stretches nearly halfway around the world. It is the third-largest continent. The land covers more than nine million square miles (24 million square kilometers). But the southern tip is only 31 miles (50 kilometers) across! It would only take about 30 minutes to drive that distance on a highway.

North America's Fast Facts
Land area: 9.3 million square miles (24.2 million square kilometers)
Population: 565,000,000
Three most common languages: English, Spanish, and French
Number of countries: 23
Largest country: Canada, 3.8 million square miles (9.9 million square kilometers)
Smallest country: St. Kitts and Nevis, 101 square miles (261 square kilometers)
Largest city: Mexico City, Mexico, population 21,000,000
Lowest elevation: Death Valley, California, U.S., 282 feet (86 meters) below sea level
Highest elevation: Mount McKinley, Alaska, U.S., 20,320 feet (6,194 meters)

Mount McKinley, Alaska, U.S.

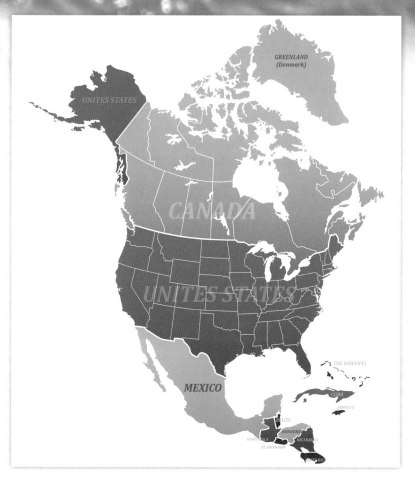

Twenty-three countries and 13 territories make up the continent. Canada, the United States of America, and Mexico are the three largest countries. The region of Central America is made of seven small countries south of Mexico. Thirteen countries from the 7,000 Caribbean islands are all part of North America. From farms to cities, tropics to the Arctic, you'll find a lot of variety on the continent.

WILDLIFE AND WILD WEATHER

What's the weather like in North America? It depends on where you are. Cold winds blow in the north. Travel south and you'll be in the hot tropics.

Wild animals and plants of all kinds live in North America. Where they live depends on the climate.

Northern Canada and most of Greenland are in the Arctic Circle. It's so cold some of the land is permanently frozen! No trees grow in the tundra.

Puerto Rican coqui frog

humpback whale

roadrunner

pronghorn

OPEN SOON

Extreme Weather

Blizzards blow long and hard in Canada and the northern United States. Tropical storms and hurricanes challenge countries and territories to the south. Heavy rains and hard winds cause deadly flooding and damage. Strong winds spread wildfires in California and other parts of the U.S.

The frozen tundra seems empty. What lives there? The snowy owl and caribou make it their habitat. Moss and **lichens** provide food for animals during the short summer thaw.

Southern Canada and most of the United States have **temperate** climates. The weather changes from day to day and from season to season. Animals such as black bears, red foxes, and mourning doves live there.

Lichen, shown here, are a food source for caribou and musk oxen in the tundra.

Despite its name, many plants and animals make Death Valley their home.

The southwestern U.S. and some of Mexico have desert climates. Death Valley is the hottest and driest place in North America. But it's home to over 1,000 plant species and nearly 500 kinds of animals. They're designed for the desert climate. Rock lady flowers and the salt creek pupfish live in Death Valley. They are not found anywhere else in the world.

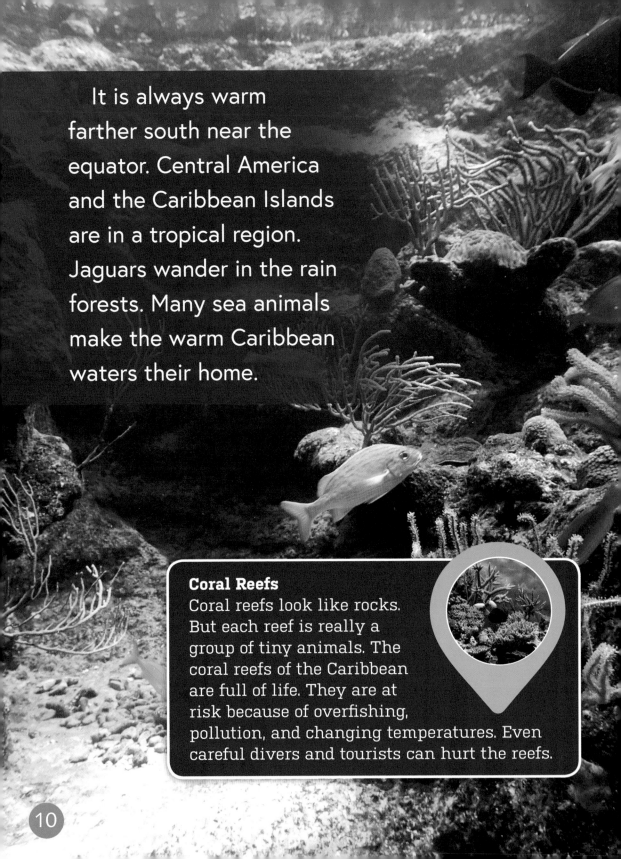

It is always warm farther south near the equator. Central America and the Caribbean Islands are in a tropical region. Jaguars wander in the rain forests. Many sea animals make the warm Caribbean waters their home.

Coral Reefs

Coral reefs look like rocks. But each reef is really a group of tiny animals. The coral reefs of the Caribbean are full of life. They are at risk because of overfishing, pollution, and changing temperatures. Even careful divers and tourists can hurt the reefs.

Pine trees grow tall in a Canadian rain forest.

Forests cover a lot of North America. Boreal, evergreen, deciduous, and rain forests are some of the continent's wooded areas.

Cloud forests have low clouds and fog. They are habitats to many unique species. They provide drinking water for people and animals. Fair-trade coffee grows in the cloud forests of Central America.

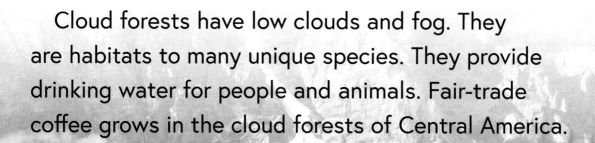

Fair-Trade Coffee

Some farmers grow coffee in a way that doesn't hurt the environment. They pay their workers a fair wage. They don't allow children to work. They sell their coffee as a "fair-trade" product. Consumers around the world know their fair-trade purchase helps small farmers and their workers.

More Fast Facts
Smallest bird in the world:
bee hummingbird of Cuba, 2.4
inches (61 millimeters) long
**Largest fresh water lake in the
world:** Lake Superior, 31,700
square miles (82,100 square
kilometers)
Most rainfall in one minute: Unionville,
Maryland, U.S. 1.23 inches (3.12 centimeters) on
July 4, 1956
Biggest island in the world: Greenland at 836,000
square miles (2,165,000 square kilometers)

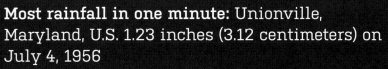

About 350 people live in Kangaamiut on Greenland's western coast.

WHAT'S THE LAND LIKE?

Glaciers carved most of the land in North America. They formed mountains, canyons, and flat areas.

The Rocky Mountains stretch about 3,000 miles (4,800 kilometers) from New Mexico into British Columbia, Canada. Many of the Sierra Madre mountains and other mountains in Mexico and Central America are actually volcanoes. Some of the volcanoes are inactive. Others are still active.

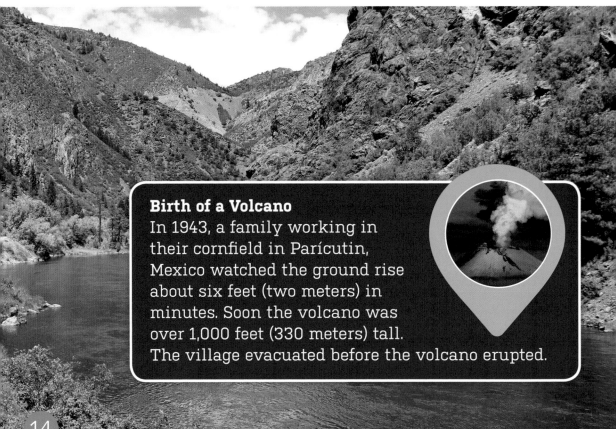

Birth of a Volcano
In 1943, a family working in their cornfield in Parícutin, Mexico watched the ground rise about six feet (two meters) in minutes. Soon the volcano was over 1,000 feet (330 meters) tall. The village evacuated before the volcano erupted.

Few European settlers lived west of the Mississippi River until the westward expansion of the United States in the 1800s.

The Great Plains sit between the Rocky Mountains and the Mississippi River. The area is known for rich soil and flat land. Farmers grow a lot of wheat and corn there.

Lakes and long rivers mark the land. The Mississippi is the longest river at 2,340 miles (3,766 kilometers). It begins in Minnesota and flows south. It empties into the Gulf of Mexico.

THE EARLIEST PEOPLE

Millions of people lived in North America before Europeans arrived. Scientists think the first people came to the continent from Asia. We call them **indigenous** people because they were the first people to live in the area. Their **descendants** became the American Indians.

Heebe-tee-tse of the Shoshone Nation, circa 1899.

Some people settled in what is now Alaska. Others migrated down the Pacific Coast. Some traveled inland. Groups of people spread throughout the main continent and islands of North America. They built communities and formed tribes.

America's Forgotten City
Cahokia was one of the world's largest cities. As many as 20,000 American Indians lived there in 1200 CE. Planners designed the city with about 80 earthen pyramids. The tallest mound is ten stories high! You can visit the historic site today in Illinois, United States.

Mayans and Aztecs built cities in lands we now call Mexico, Guatemala, and Belize. They built **canals**, apartment-like buildings, and even pyramids. Some people lived in villages. Other groups were nomadic. That means they moved around the land.

A Long Legacy
The native people around Mexico were advanced societies. The Mayans excelled in science and math. Many scholars believe they invented the number zero. The Aztecs used irrigation in their farming practices. They were also the first to chew gum. The Mayans and the Aztecs both enjoyed the first chocolate drinks.

The ancient architecture of the Mayan ruins still stand today.

A MULTICULTURAL HISTORY AND HERITAGE

Explorers from Europe found the New World. Soon the European countries wanted to own the land. They began building settlements and **colonies** in America in the 1500s.

Spain claimed a lot of North American land for

Christopher Columbus arrived in the Bahamas in 1492.

its own. So did France, Portugal, and England. Other countries like Sweden and the Netherlands took land, too.

Erik the Red
Erik the Red was a Viking from Norway. He explored southern Greenland. Then he persuaded others to join him at his new colony. It was the first European settlement in North America, around 986. His son, Leif Erikson, also explored North America long before Christopher Columbus.

The Europeans even claimed land where American Indians already lived. The American Indians were forced to leave. The European settlers moved onto their lands. They built colonies.

The colonies were ruled by distant countries until the 18th and 19th centuries. Then much of North America became independent nations instead of colonies.

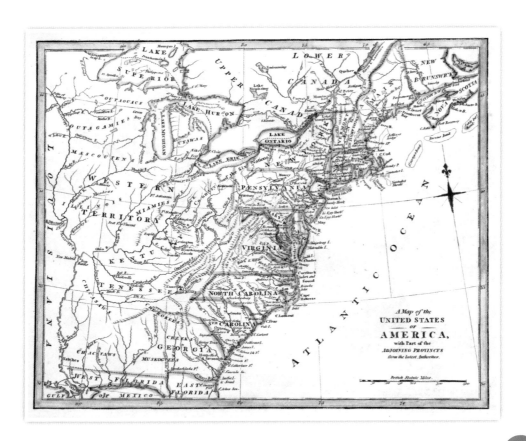

But that didn't help everyone. The governments of new countries, like the United States and Canada, controlled the fate of the American Indians. Slaves had been brought from Africa from the 1500s to the 1800s. They were forced to work on **plantations** in many parts of North America. Even native groups from Central America were enslaved.

That was a long time ago. Slavery is no longer legal. But even today not everyone is treated fairly.

NORTH AMERICA TODAY

More than 565 million people live in North America. People from all over the world have moved to the continent.

Some relocate for work or education. People even move from country to country within North America. Immigrants try to build a better life in their new country.

There are many cities on the continent. Mexico City is the most populated city in North America. Its historic and modern buildings attract visitors from around the world. New York City is the largest city in the United States. It's known as the business and cultural capital of the world.

Lake City
Mexico City was built on the ruins of the Aztecs' island capital of Tenochtitlán. As the surrounding lake beds dried, the city spread. Today, the beautiful city is the largest in the Americas. But it struggles to provide clean water to all its residents.

Banana Wars
Some farms in Central America were owned by United States businesses. Employees wanted workers' rights in the late 1800s. But the U.S. military used force to stop the workers and help crop owners. These are sometimes called Banana Wars. Worker and human rights are still concerns today in Central America.

Some people live in towns. Others live in the country. In rural areas, people might drive or walk far for work, school, or even groceries.

Some North Americans are wealthy. But poverty is in every country.

Rich or poor, the people of North America celebrate. Some have private parties in homes with family. Often towns and cities host festivals open to everyone. These celebrations might honor a religious holiday or national event. Other special events celebrate a person, sport, or even a hobby.

People celebrate with music throughout the continent. The Rock & Roll Hall of Fame is in Cleveland, Ohio. Québec, Canada hosts the Montreal International Jazz Festival. Reggae music began in Jamaica. Other musical styles like hip-hop and country are also popular.

Religion is important to many people. Others do not practice a religion. Christianity is the most popular religion in North America. But all faiths are found there.

North American **industry** is strong. Minerals like copper and silver are mined. Workers drill for oil and natural gas. **Textiles** are made. Silicon Valley in California is known for its technology. Automobile, food, and wood products are also sold around the world.

Mines like this gold mine are found throughout North America.

The Panama Canal helps countries around the world trade goods. The manmade canal provides a shortcut across the land so ships don't have to go around South America.

Tourism is strong throughout the continent. It is a major industry in the Caribbean. People from around the world visit North America. They want to experience its attractions and natural beauty. North America has a lot to explore.

Fast Facts about the Construction of the Panama Canal (1904–1914)
Dynamite used: 61 million pounds (28 million kilograms)
Rock and soil excavated: 240 million cubic yards (183.5 million cubic meters)
Concrete used: 4.4 million cubic yards (3.4 million cubic meters)
Length from port to port: 51 miles (82 kilometers)
Number of workers: 56,000
Number of deaths from disease and accidents: 5,609
Cost to the U.S.: $350 million

ACTIVITY: LUMINARIES

Las Posadas, or "The Inns," is a religious celebration in Me[x]
Guatemala, and other countries. This Christmas tradition act[s]
Bible story of Mary and Joseph's journey from Nazareth to Be[thlehem]
The festivities last nine days, ending on Christmas Eve.

The people celebrating Las Posadas divide into two group[s]
innkeepers and tired travelers. The tired travelers look for a p[lace to]
rest. Luminaries made with paper bags, sand, and a candle lig[ht the]
path as they walk to the homes of friends. There, the people [pretending]
to be innkeepers tell them there is no room at the inn. After a[while,]
the innkeepers finally let the travelers into the house. Each ni[ght of Las]
Posadas ends with a feast and song.

Create your own luminary to celebrate Las Posadas!

Supplies:
- ✓ small paper bag(s)
- ✓ hole punch
- ✓ sand
- ✓ electric tea light candle
- ✓ decorative scissors, optional

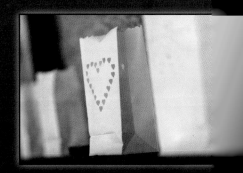

Directions:
1. Use the hole punch to create a design in the paper bag. [Make a heart]
or other symbol. Leave at least two inches (5 centimeters) a[t the bottom]
of the bag without any holes.
2. Trim a scalloped edge along the top of the bag if using de[corative]
scissors or roll the top of the bag down about an inch (2.5 ce[ntimeters),]
keeping the bag open.
3. Place sand in the bottom of the bag.
4. Turn on the electric candle and place it in the bag. It shou[ld]

RECIPE: ATOL DE ELOTE (SWEET CORN DRINK)

In El Salvador, this creamy drink is especially enjoyed at family gatherings but can be made at any time. Authentic atol is made with fresh corn. You can also make it with frozen corn that's been thawed.

Ingredients

- 16 ounces (450 grams) frozen corn or 5 ears of corn
- 3 cups (750 milliliters) milk
- 1 cinnamon stick
- ½ cup (100 grams) sugar
- ground cinnamon (for garnish)

Directions:

1. Thaw the corn or cut it off the cob.
2. Place 2 cups (500 milliliters) of milk, corn, sugar, and cinnamon stick in a blender. Cover and blend for two minutes or longer. It should be smooth.
3. Strain the mixture into a large sauce pan. (A metal strainer works best.) With the pulp in the strainer, press and stir the pulp with the back of a large spoon to drain more of the atol into the saucepan. Discard the remaining corn pulp.
4. Add 1 cup of milk (250 milliliters) to the corn mixture in the sauce pan. Simmer the mixture for 15 to 20 minutes over medium-low heat. Stir frequently to prevent burning.
5. Pour into mugs. Sprinkle with ground cinnamon. Serve warm.

GLOSSARY

canals (kuh-NALZ): channels that are dug across land so that boats or ships can travel between two bodies of water, or so that water can flow from one place to another

colonies (KAH-luh-neez): territories that have been settled by people from another country and are controlled by that country

descendants (di-SEN-duhnts): your descendants are your children, your children's children, and so on into the future

indigenous (in-DIJ-uh-nuhs): originating in a particular region or country, native

industry (IN-duh-stree): manufacturing companies and other businesses

lichens (LYE-kuhns): sponge-like growths on rocks, walls, and trees that consists of algae and fungi growing close together

plantations (plant-TAY-shuhns): a large farm found in warm climates where crops such as coffee, rubber, and cotton are grown

temperate (TEM-per-it): if an area has a temperate climate, the temperature is rarely very high or very low

textiles (TEK-stiles): woven or knitted fabric or cloth

tourism (TOOR-iz-uhm): the business of providing activities and accommodation to tourists

INDEX

SHOW WHAT YOU KNOW

1. Who were the first people in North America?

2. What lives in the hottest place in North America?

3. Why did European countries establish colonies?

4. Name three North American industries.

5. How does the Panama Canal help people throughout the world?

FURTHER READING

Petersen, Christine, *Learning about North America*, Lerner Publications, 2016.

Koenig, Emily, *North America*, ABDO Publishing Company, 2014.

Daly, Ruth, *The Natural World: North America*, AV2 by Weigl, 2015.

ABOUT THE AUTHOR

Annette Whipple lives in Pennsylvania with her husband and three children. She strives to inspire a sense of wonder in young people while exciting them about science, social studies, and writing. When she's not writing, Annette enjoys reading a good book and cooking new foods, like her cousin's atol recipe. Learn more about Annette, her books, and her presentations at www.AnnetteWhipple.com.

Meet the Author!
www.meetREMauthors.com

www.rourkeeducationalmedia.com

PHOTO CREDITS: Cover & Title Pg ©NASA, ©Nicolas McComber, ©searagen, ©espiegle, ©Vadim_Nefedov, ©BirdImages, Top Pg Bar ©fergregory, Pg 4 ©joannasgallery, Pg 5 ©kateukraine,Pg 6 ©ilikestudio, ©Yann hubert, ©NaturesMomentsuk, ©Birdiegal, Pg 7 ©Trong Nguyen, ©Zoran Ras, Pg 8 ©By Sergey Privalov, Pg 9 ©stanic8, Pg 10 ©Kwiatek7, ©Dobermaraner, Pg 11 ©Chad Zuber, Pg 12 ©TRphotos, ©Ilja Generalov, Pg 13 ©Melinda Fawver, ©MicheleB, Pg 14 ©Cristobal Garciaferro, ©Tupungato, Pg 15 ©Nancy Bauer, Pg 16 ©Everett Historical, Pg 17 ©By Everett Collection, ©Joseph Sohm, Pg 18 ©Irina Klyuchnikova, ©Carla Nichiata, Pg 19 ©DC_Aperture, Pg 20 ©Pavel Tvrdy, ©Everett Historical, Pg 21 ©I. Pilon, Pg 22 ©Everett Historical, Pg 23 ©Fabio Imhoff, Pg 24 ©a katz, ©Hanna_photo, Pg 25 ©AGCuesta, Pg 26 ©Wollertz, Pg 27 ©Galina Savina, Pg 28 ©AleksandarGeorgiev, Pg 29 ©Superheang168

Edited by: Keli Sipperley
Cover design by: Rhea Magaro-Wallace
Interior design by: Corey Mills

Library of Congress PCN Data

North America / Annette Whipple
 (Earth's Continents)
 ISBN 978-1-64156-409-0 (hard cover)
 ISBN 978-1-64156-535-6 (soft cover)
 ISBN 978-1-64156-659-9 (e-Book)
Library of Congress Control Number: 2018930430

Rourke Educational Media
Printed in the United States of America,
North Mankato, Minnesota